Dream horse . . . or nightmare?

I was about to meet my horse! I crossed my fingers. If I couldn't have a tall black horse, I thought a tall white horse would do.

"This is Ranger, Jessie," Diana said. She opened the stall door.

I looked in. . . .

The horse looking back at me wasn't tall. He was short and chunky.

He *was* black—but only in spots. He was also white—in spots.

"Isn't he something?" Diana asked.

"He's something," I agreed. I just wasn't sure *what*. "Um, what is he, exactly?" I asked her.

"Ranger is an Appaloosa," said Diana. "It's a breed of horse from the Old West."

"Are you sure he's not a Dalmatian?" I asked. "He has the same spots."

Diana laughed.

But I didn't see anything funny about it. Ranger couldn't have been less like my dream horse if he had tried!

Don't miss any of the books in
this fabulous new series!

And look for this other great series
from HarperPaperbacks:

PONY CAMP

Jessie Takes the Reins

SUSAN SAUNDERS

HarperPaperbacks

A Division of HarperCollins*Publishers*

This is a work of fiction. The characters, incidents, and dialogues are products of the author's imagination and are not to be construed as real. Any resemblance to actual events or persons, living or dead, is entirely coincidental.

HarperPaperbacks   A Division of HarperCollinsPublishers
                    10 East 53rd Street, New York, N.Y. 10022

Copyright © 1994 by Susan Saunders and Daniel Weiss Associates, Inc.
Cover art copyright © 1994 Daniel Weiss Associates, Inc.

Produced by Daniel Weiss Associates, Inc., 33 West 17th Street, New York, New York 10011.

First printing: April 1994

Printed in the United States of America

HarperPaperbacks and colophon are trademarks of HarperCollinsPublishers

10 9 8 7 6 5 4 3

1

"*Pony camp!*" Just saying the words out loud gave me goose bumps. I grabbed my brand-new riding hat and plopped it onto my head. "I'm going to pony camp, and it's about time, too."

I smiled at myself in my bedroom mirror. "It only took me eight and a half years to get a horse!"

I'm Jessie Johnson. For most of my eight and a half years, I've been crazy about horses.

When I was a baby, my favorite stories were always horse stories. My favorite toy was a stuffed horse named Lady.

I started collecting little glass horses when I was five. Now I have forty-one of them.

But the main thing I have always wanted is a *real* horse.

I asked for a horse every Christmas and every birthday since I could talk. "If I can have a horse, I'll never ask you for another thing," I promised my parents.

"Horses are too expensive," Dad would say. "Do you have any idea how much they eat?"

"Half a bale of hay and a coffee can of oats a day," I'd answer. I've read every horse book in the library, so I'm an expert on horses.

But Dad was never impressed with how much I knew about horses. He would say, "I could feed this family for what it would cost to have a horse!"

"I'll give up my allowance for the rest of my life," I told him.

But he would frown and shake his head.

Mom would say stuff like, "Even if we

could afford to feed a horse, Jessie, where would we put it?"

"The garden shed is big enough," I would say. "For a small horse, anyway."

"Yeah, right. And then who has to clean up the mess in the backyard?" Michael would growl. Michael is my older brother, and he can be a real pain. "Not me! I mow the lawn, and that's all!"

I couldn't convince them, no matter what I said. . . .

Until a couple of weeks ago, just before school was over.

This past year I was a third grader at Westbrook Elementary. I got pretty good grades, even in math.

So I was kind of surprised when Dad said one evening, "Jessie, your mom and I want to talk to you. Please come into the living room."

The living room is where we always go to talk about important things.

"Sit down on the couch," Mom said,

and she looked really serious.

Now I was getting worried. Had I done something wrong?

"Honey, we've signed you up for a new kind of camp this summer," Dad said.

"What about Camp Ogunquit?" I asked.

Ogunquit is the day camp that my best friend, Pam Werner, and I have gone to for the last three summers. We swim and hike and do sports, and I like it there.

"This is a different kind of camp," Mom said.

My heart sank. "Sleep-away camp?" I asked.

Okay, I *am* eight and a half. But I'm not ready for sleep-away camp yet. I thought maybe Mom and Dad were tired of me nagging them for a horse all the time. Maybe they wanted a vacation from me.

But Dad said, "No, not sleep-away."

Not sleep-away? What other kinds of camps were there?

"It's not a math camp, is it? Or a computer

camp?" I asked nervously. I was feeling worse and worse. "I mean, summer is supposed to be fun. Isn't it?"

Then I saw that Dad was starting to grin. "You're not even close," he said.

"I'm surprised at you, Jessie," Mom added. "What have you been asking for all these years?"

"A horse?" I screamed. "You're getting me a horse?"

"Hold on!" Dad was laughing now. "No, we are not getting you a horse. . . ."

"But we hope you'll like this almost as much," Mom said. "We signed you up for eight weeks at Horizon Hills Farm!"

"What's Horizon Hills Farm?" I asked.

"It's a *pony* camp!" Dad said. "You'll learn all about riding horses and grooming them . . ."

"And you'll have the same horse for the whole summer," Mom said.

"Oh, wow! You guys are the greatest!" I said, giving them each a big hug. My own horse for eight whole weeks! I could hardly believe it.

Then I had an upsetting thought. "But Pam is going back to Camp Ogunquit," I said sadly.

"Maybe not," said Dad. "We told Pam's parents about Horizon Hills, and—"

Suddenly the phone rang. It was Pam. "Of course I'll go to Horizon Hills, too," she said. "I'm not spending the whole summer by myself!"

Now everything was perfect.

Over the next two weeks, I read the pony camp program so many times that I'd memorized it: "Morning, 9:00 to 12:00: riding lessons and horse care. Students are grouped as beginners, intermediates, and advanced riders."

I was just a beginner, but I was sure that wouldn't last long. Anyone who knew as much as I did about horses would move up pretty quickly.

Next the program said: "Lunch under the

trees, 12:00 to 1:00. Swimming, canoeing, and crafts in the Red Barn, 1:00 to 4:00."

The only thing that could have been better was "Riding, 9:00 to 4:00."

Mom took me to the store. She bought me a riding hat, which looks sort of like a baseball cap, except it's hard, like a bike helmet. It had a strap to hold it on, under my chin.

She also bought me riding jeans and a braided leather belt. Best of all, I got a white shirt with a high collar for horse shows. I couldn't wait to ride in horse shows and win all those ribbons.

And finally the first day of pony camp was here!

I opened my closet door. I took out the riding boots my granddad had sent me. They looked great—they were made of dark-brown leather. They even smelled good.

While I was getting dressed, I imagined myself sitting on the back of a huge Thoroughbred. He would be black, with a long mane and tail. He would be named something like . . . Thunder!

I closed my eyes for a second. Thunder and I were racing across a field at Horizon Hills Farm. We practically flew over a tall stone fence. I sat proudly in the saddle as I got my blue ribbon. I was a perfect rider. . . .

"Jessie!" Mom called from downstairs. "Breakfast! If you don't hurry, we'll be late!"

Late? No way! I didn't want to miss one single second of pony camp.

I tugged my boots on over my riding jeans. I checked myself out again in the mirror. I looked like a pro!

Then I galloped downstairs.

"Here's a bowl for your cereal," Mom said when I clattered into the kitchen.

"Or you could just eat them out of that bowl on your head." Michael snickered.

He meant my riding hat.

But I didn't even bother to make a face at him.

Who cared about Michael? Today was the start of a whole new life!

2

Pam was waiting on her front steps when Mom and I drove up that morning.

Pam is a great friend. I know she isn't crazy about horses. In fact, she doesn't even like big dogs. But we always do everything together. And I was sure I could make her like pony camp as much as I did.

"Hi, Mrs. Johnson," Pam said. She slid into the backseat of our car.

"Hey—you look sharp," she said to me.

"So do you," I said. "Great hat."

Pam's riding hat was navy blue with white stars on it.

"Thanks. I tried on so many of them yesterday at Boots and Saddles that I got a headache," she said. Pam is a super shopper. "One thing I definitely like about pony camp is the clothes," she added.

Horizon Hills Farm is outside of Jamestown. That's the town next to Westbrook, where we live. As Mom turned onto the highway, Pam said, "Do you think anyone from school will be at this place?"

"No matter who's there, the Dream Team will blow them away," I told her. "As usual." The Dream Team is what Pam and I call ourselves sometimes.

I'm really good at sports. Pam is good, too. And we've played together for so long that we're almost a team by ourselves.

In softball, if I'm pitcher, Pam is catcher. In basketball, Pam does lay-ups, and I do jump shots. In volleyball, I set the ball up, and Pam spikes it.

We get picked first for all the teams at school.

Some of the kids are always the last to be picked. I would die of embarrassment! Although it didn't seem to bother Maxine Brown. . . .

Maxine was new at Westbrook Elementary this past year. Sometimes I wondered where she went to school before. Where in the world is there a school with kids who don't like sports?

Maxine acted as if getting wrinkled or sweaty or dusty was stupid. She even told Pam once that sports were dumb. Just thinking about it now made me glad that I wouldn't have to see Maxine until school started again.

"I can't believe Maxine Brown thinks sports are dumb," I said to Pam.

"Maybe she just says that because she's not good at them," Pam said.

"Maybe." I had never thought of that before. "Anyway, *she* definitely won't be at Horizon Hills."

"We'll meet lots of new kids," Pam said. "Maybe even some new boys."

Pam and I have been going to school with the same old boys for four years.

But I'm not very interested in boys. "I just want to meet horses," I said.

"Yeah." Pam looked thoughtful. "I hope my horse likes me."

Pam worries a lot, especially about new stuff.

"Everybody likes you," I told her. It's true—Pam is so nice that she makes friends with everyone.

I wasn't a bit worried. I already knew a lot about riding. As soon as I got on a horse, there would be no stopping me!

"Girls, this fence is the beginning of Horizon Hills Farm," Mom said from the front seat.

I sat up straight to stare out the window. "Wow, look at that!" I said to Pam.

At the edge of a field, a horse and rider jumped over a high stone wall. It looked easy and smooth, almost like floating.

Pam caught her breath. "That is so cool!" she said.

"We'll be doing that soon," I told her.

"I don't know—it looks pretty hard," Pam said. And Mom agreed with her.

"Riding isn't easy, Jessie," Mom warned. "Learning to jump may take a while."

But I didn't pay attention to them. I was sure I was only a week or two away from floating over fences.

Mom turned the car into a long, winding driveway. We drove by a large pen, where wooden jumps were set up. Jumps look like pieces of fence. As you can guess from the name, horses jump over them.

We passed two outdoor riding rings. Then we pulled up next to a huge barn lined with windows.

Some of the windows were open. Several horses had stuck their heads out: two big chestnuts—a chestnut is a reddish-brown horse—with blond manes and tails, and a small brown horse.

15

In the window closest to us was a tall black horse. When we got out of the car, he looked us over carefully.

I pointed to the black horse. "That one is going to be mine!" I said to Pam. "I just know it—he's exactly like my dream horse."

Suddenly the black horse bobbed its head up and down and whinnied. It seemed to be talking to me!

"See? He knows it, too," I said with a giggle.

Then a large man with a tan face walked out of the barn. He came over to us.

"This is Mr. Morgan," Mom told us. "He and his wife own Horizon Hills Farm."

"Mrs. Johnson! Good to see you," Mr. Morgan said. "This must be Jessie. And this is . . ."

"Pam Werner," Mom told him.

"Welcome to pony camp," said Mr. Morgan.

"Excuse me, I have a question," Pam said shyly. "Will we really be riding ponies? I'm kind of tall. . . ."

Mr. Morgan shook his head and smiled. "You're probably thinking of Shetland ponies. We do have a few very small ponies for the youngest children. But 'pony' really means any horse under fourteen and a half hands."

"Hands?" Pam asked, puzzled.

"Horses are measured from the bottom of a front hoof to the top of their shoulder," Mr. Morgan explained. "And they have always been measured with the human hand."

He held out his hand so that his thumb was on top. "One hand is the distance across the palm from one side to the other."

"But everybody's hands are different sizes," Pam said. She was looking at Mr. Morgan's hand, and then at her own.

"Right," said Mr. Morgan. "So one hand has come to mean four inches. A pony is any horse under fifty-eight inches at the shoulder."

"Pam, I could have told you that!" I whispered. I hoped she would catch on fast at

17

Horizon Hills and not embarrass the Dream Team!

"Girls, why don't we go inside and meet the rest of your group?" Mr. Morgan said." And your 'ponies,' of course."

3

We were going to meet our horses! I had been waiting for eight and a half years to meet my horse. I had never been so excited in my life!

I felt like jumping up and down. But I didn't want to embarrass myself. So I just squeezed Pam's arm for a second.

"Pam's dad will pick you up at four," Mom told us. She was getting ready to leave.

I grabbed my tote bag and my lunch out of the car.

"Have a great time," Mom said.

"The best!" I said.

Then Pam and I followed Mr. Morgan into the barn.

The barn was cool and shady inside. It seemed to stretch on forever.

"This is our tack room," Mr. Morgan said.

"'Tack' means saddles and bridles," I whispered to Pam before she could ask another dumb question.

Mr. Morgan pointed to a wall covered with ribbons and prizes from horse shows. "Those were all won by our campers," he said proudly.

Next came an indoor riding ring. A teenage girl in purple leggings was riding a brown horse. As we watched, the horse walked sideways all the way across the ring. It lifted its feet high in the air.

"He looks like he's dancing!" Pam said.

"This kind of riding is called *dressage*," Mr. Morgan said. "Sara has been a Horizon Hills camper for ten years now. She's a blue-ribbon winner at all the shows."

"That looks really hard," Pam said to me.

"I wonder if we'll ever win blue ribbons."

"Absolutely!" I said. "We'll be winning ribbons in no time at all."

I was sure *I* would be, at least.

On the far side of the ring, there was a long hallway lined with horse stalls.

"This hall is called an alley," I told Pam.

"How do you know?" she asked.

"I read it in a book," I said proudly. I was sure I would be the smartest camper in my group.

The alley was jammed with kids. It looked a lot like the halls at school—a bunch of kids crowded together, all talking at the same time. But instead of wearing sneakers and caps, all these kids had on boots and riding hats.

Pam and I followed Mr. Morgan down the alley. We heard campers saying things like, "I'm braiding Lady's tail in a french braid for the show." And, "Boomer refused the fence—I almost fell off!" And, "George thinks I'm ready to start eventing."

21

"The only thing I understood was about the french braid!" Pam said nervously. "What is eventing?"

"Eventing is riding a horse on a cross-country course," I told her. I couldn't wait to do that myself!

I didn't see anyone I knew in the alley. But I wasn't really looking at the kids. I was a lot more interested in looking over the stall doors at the horses. There were tall horses, short horses, gray horses, chestnut horses, and a few bays. Bay horses are tan or a rich, red-brown color, with a black mane and tail—and the bays were even prettier than they had looked in my horse books! But best of all was the black horse I had already seen.

Up close, he was shiny and sleek, with a long mane. He looked just like the horse I had always imagined myself riding!

"Mr. Morgan, can I ride this one?" I asked. I read his name off a sign on the stall door: SASHA.

Mr. Morgan smiled. "Sasha is too much

horse for a beginner to handle," he said. "Maybe in a year or two."

"A year or two?" I said. I shook my head. "No way. I always catch on quick in sports."

I reached up to pat Sasha's soft nose on the way by. "You'll be mine soon," I whispered to him.

"We have to find your instructor," Mr. Morgan was saying. "There she is . . . Diana!"

Diana was small and thin. She had light-brown hair pulled back into a thick braid. She was wearing cream-colored riding pants and knee-high black boots.

"She looks nice," Pam said to me.

Diana waved us toward her with a friendly grin.

"Here are two of your students, Diana. This is Jessie Johnson, and this is Pam Werner," Mr. Morgan said. "Jessie and Pam, this is Diana Kirk—a very fine rider indeed."

"Great to meet you!" Diana gave us both hugs. "This is another member of our group, Peter Brody."

"Where?" I asked. I didn't see a boy anywhere near us.

"Now, where did he go?" Diana said. She was looking around, too. "Uh-oh! He's getting candy again."

A pudgy boy was pulling a knob on a candy machine in the far corner of the barn.

"Peter!" Diana called. "Your parents said no snacks, remember? Could you please join us?"

The boy gave the candy machine a smack with his hand. Then he slowly turned around.

Peter looked a little older than Pam and me. Peter also looked messy. His shirt was hanging out of his riding pants. And he had chocolate smeared on his face.

His sandy hair was shaved halfway up his head. It had been trimmed into a bowl cut.

"With that haircut, what will he look like with his riding hat on?" Pam wondered out loud.

"Totally bald," I said. I started giggling.

Pam tried not to giggle. But she couldn't help herself, either.

We were still giggling when Peter stomped over to us, frowning.

"Peter, this is Pam and Jessie," Diana said.

"Hi," I said, pulling myself together.

"Hi," said Pam.

Peter didn't bother to say anything. He raised his eyes toward the ceiling and groaned softly.

"As soon as the fourth member of our group shows up, we can get started," Diana said.

The crowd of kids was thinning out. Diana stood on tiptoe to peer over the campers' heads.

"I think that's her coming down the alley," Diana said. "Yes . . . Maxine, we're over here!"

Maxine? "Maxine isn't a very popular name. . . ." I said to Pam.

"I hope it isn't the Maxine from West-brook Elementary," Pam said. "She's so neat! She always makes me feel like a total slob."

"It better not be!" I said. "Maxine Brown is so bad at sports, she would hold us all back!" I didn't want to waste any time at pony camp. I wanted to be riding Sasha as soon as possible!

"It can't be the Maxine we know," Pam said. "Not with all this dust and dirt."

But it *was* Maxine Brown heading right toward us.

She looked as though she had just popped out of a dry-cleaning machine, along with her riding clothes. She was perfect from top to bottom. Not one blond hair was out of place on her head. Not a speck of dust dared to stick to her riding boots.

"Maxine," Diana began, "this is—"

But Maxine said, "I know. Jessie and Pam."

She wrinkled her nose as though she smelled something weird.

"You're already friends?" Diana asked

happily. "Excellent! We're going to have a great summer!"

"Great," Pam said in a low voice. She was smoothing down her shirt and combing her short brown hair with her fingers. Then she tried to shine the tips of her boots on the back of her riding pants.

"Where's Peter?" Diana asked, suddenly frowning. "Peter!" she called out.

Peter Brody had disappeared again.

I sighed. I hadn't expected to spend the whole, entire summer with the prissiest girl at Westbrook Elementary. Not to mention a fat, cranky boy.

Then I shrugged. So what? Pam was here with me. And, most important, I would have a horse!

"Three girls!" Peter Brody suddenly mumbled from behind me. It was the first time he had spoken. I could hardly understand him because he had a giant sour ball tucked into his cheek.

"Yuck," Peter added.

4

"**P**eter and Maxine already have their lockers. I'll show you two where yours are," Diana said to Pam and me. "You can store your totes in them."

Before Peter could sneak off again, Diana told him to come with us. "You left your riding hat in your locker," she reminded him.

"Do I have to wear it?" Peter grumbled. "It makes me look like a geek."

I elbowed Pam, and she grinned at me. We were pretty sure Peter was right.

"We're not going to do any major riding on the first day, anyway," Peter added.

"We aren't going to ride today?" I cried. I had no time to lose—Sasha was waiting!

"Today you'll get to know your horses. You'll learn how to groom them, and how to saddle and bridle them," Diana told me. And to Peter she added, "Anytime you're working with horses, you have to wear the hat. Those are the rules."

"What should I do?" Maxine asked Diana. Maxine was already wearing her riding hat. It was black, with a hot-pink trim. It looked perfect with her beautiful riding clothes.

"You know where Winnie's stall is. You can lead her to the indoor ring if you like," Diana said to Maxine. "We'll meet you there."

The rest of us started up the alley.

"Has Maxine been here before?" Pam asked Diana.

"She started taking lessons a couple of months ago," Diana said. "I have a feeling Maxine is a natural."

"Maxine Brown? You have to be kidding!"

I said. Then I put my hand over my mouth. I hadn't meant to sound so nasty, but it just slipped out.

Luckily, there was so much noise in the barn that Diana didn't hear me—I didn't want her to think I was mean.

But I had seen Maxine on the baseball field and the volleyball court. The girl was terrible at sports!

"If Maxine Brown is a natural, then I'm the best rider who ever lived," I whispered to Pam. "And so are you."

"I'll settle for not falling off," Pam said.

Pam was definitely nervous about riding. Not me—I couldn't wait!

The lockers were in Mr. Morgan's office, on the far side of the tack room. While Pam and I stuffed our totes and lunches into empty lockers, Peter jammed his riding hat onto his head.

It looked pretty silly. All of Peter's hair was covered by the hat. Everything below the hat was shaved clean.

"His head looks like a bowling ball!" I murmured to Pam.

Peter caught us giggling again.

"See?" he growled to Diana. "They think I look like a dork."

"The hat stays on, Peter," Diana said. "Let's go find our horses."

As we followed Diana out of the tack room, a tall, stringy boy crashed into Peter. He obviously did it on purpose.

"You *are* a dork, Bullethead," said the boy. He had a raspy voice and a nasty grin.

Peter ignored him, and the boy headed into the tack room.

But Peter's face and neck were bright red, from the edge of his hat down to his shirt collar.

"Who was that?" I asked Peter.

"A kid from my school," Peter mumbled. "Kevin Harris."

"He's not very nice," Pam said softly.

"No kidding!" Peter said. He looked grateful. "His sister is as bad as he is," Peter added.

"Here we are," Diana said. She stopped in front of a stall door. "Our horses are right in a row."

She opened the first door. "Pam, your horse is named Gracie," Diana said.

Gracie was a chestnut-colored horse with a white streak down her face and two white feet.

Gracie was sound asleep. And a small calico cat was curled up on Gracie's back. The cat was asleep, too.

Diana lifted the cat down.

"This is Jane," Diana told us. "She lives in the barn, and she likes Gracie's stall the best. Some people think cats help horses to stay calm."

I thought Jane had made Gracie *too* calm. The mare didn't even open her eyes until Diana snapped a leather strap to her halter. A halter is a harness that fits around a horse's head so that you can lead it.

Then Gracie yawned, showing a mouthful of giant, yellow teeth.

"I hope my horse is livelier," I said.

But Pam didn't seem to mind a lazy horse. "Calm is fine with me," she said.

Pam held on to the leather halter strap. Jane rubbed against her legs. Gracie yawned again.

Peter and I followed Diana to the next stall.

"This is your horse, Peter," Diana said. "His name is Hogan."

Hogan was sort of rust colored. He was bulky, with a big round stomach.

Hogan's mane was shaved close to his neck—sort of a horse version of a bowl cut.

And Hogan was snacking. Diana really had to tug on his halter to get his head out of the feed bucket.

Peter and Hogan already had a few things in common: haircuts and eating habits.

Diana and I left Hogan chewing and Peter sucking on another giant sour ball.

The next horse would be mine! I crossed my fingers. If I couldn't have a tall black horse, I thought a tall white horse would do. Or even a dark-brown one.

"And this is Ranger, Jessie," Diana said. She opened the third door.

I looked in . . .

The horse looking back at me wasn't tall. He was short and chunky.

He *was* black—but only in spots. He was also white—in spots.

"Isn't he something?" Diana asked cheerfully.

"He's something," I agreed. I just wasn't sure *what*. "Um, what is he, exactly?" I asked her.

"Ranger is an Appaloosa," said Diana. "It's a breed of horse from the Old West."

"Are you sure he's not a Dalmatian?" I asked. "He has the same spots." I could have added, "And the same ears," because Ranger's ears were so big that they were almost floppy.

Diana laughed.

But I didn't see anything funny about it.

Ranger couldn't have been less like my dream horse if he had tried.

He didn't seem to think much of me, either.

He took a good, long look at me. Then he shifted his rear end around so his stubby tail was pointed toward us.

"Ranger, stop that," Diana said firmly.

Then she said to me, "First lesson: Don't walk up to a horse from behind. You might surprise him, and then you could get kicked."

She slapped Ranger lightly on the rump.

When he curved his neck around to see what was going on, Diana grabbed his halter. Then she pulled him back to the front of the stall.

"Sometimes Ranger is grumpy about leaving his stall," Diana told me.

She hooked a strap to his halter. She handed the other end of the strap to me.

Ranger and I stared at each other for a second.

Okay, so what if Ranger wasn't exactly what I had had in mind? He was still a horse, right?

Right. He would do for a few days—until I worked up to Sasha, I thought. And I felt a lot better.

"Jessie, you can lead Ranger forward now," Diana said.

I faced Ranger. I pulled hard on the strap with both hands.

Ranger jerked his head up in the air. Then he backed up so fast that he nearly pulled me down!

"Whoa!" I said. What else can you say to a horse?

Ranger rolled his eyes and snorted.

"What happened?" I asked Diana.

"Second lesson: When you're leading a horse, don't face him," Diana replied. "Ranger thought you were moving toward him. He didn't want to step on you by walking forward himself."

"That makes sense," I said.

I turned around so that I faced away from Ranger.

"Keep to his left," Diana said.

Suddenly I felt something thump against my riding hat. I hopped sideways just before Ranger pressed his nose against my hat again.

"He's checking you out," Diana said with a smile. "Keep both hands on the strap. Now walk toward the stall door."

Slowly, Ranger and I followed Diana into the alley.

I guess I had been holding my breath, because all of a sudden I let it out with a whoosh.

"My first step on the way to a blue ribbon," I whispered.

5

Almost every horse in the barn was lined up in the indoor ring. And every camper at Horizon Hills held a big brush.

We were grooming our horses.

Ranger and I were standing next to Pam and Gracie, who were next to Peter and Hogan. Maxine was at the end with her mare, Winnie.

I took a long swipe at Ranger's shoulder. It raised a thick cloud of dust, and I sneezed.

"Maxine Brown's parents probably made

her come here," I said to Pam. "She must hate this dirt."

I knelt under Ranger's stomach to look at Maxine.

Okay, so I was wrong. Maxine didn't seem to mind the dirt at all. In fact, she was raising a cloud of it on Winnie—and looking as though she enjoyed every minute of it.

Winnie was a dainty gray horse with a darker-gray mane and tail. Maxine was combing Winnie's forelock—that's the long piece of hair that hangs down between a horse's ears.

I stared at Maxine from under Ranger's stomach. I couldn't understand why she looked so comfortable around horses when she always looked so uncomfortable doing other sports. All of a sudden, Ranger nipped at me! His teeth closed with a click on the side of my shirt, and he tugged.

You can bet that I stood up fast!

"Cut that out!" I yelled. "Diana, Ranger tried to bite me!"

"Ranger is just being playful," Diana said.

But I wasn't so sure. "I think this horse has an attitude problem," I said to Pam in a low voice.

Ranger was starting to make me a little jumpy.

Then Maxine interrupted. "If you tie his head closer to the railing, he won't be able to reach you," she said.

"Maybe you should do what she said," Pam whispered to me.

"I had already thought of that myself," I said angrily. "Would you take sports advice from a girl who strikes out every time she's at bat?"

But I tied Ranger closer to the railing. And he didn't nip at me again.

"I'm going to get your saddles and bridles so we can tack up our horses," Diana said. She went down the alley toward the tack room. Before she came back, four intermediate campers—two girls and two boys—led their horses right past us.

43

The first girl stopped in front of Maxine. "Hi, Maxine," she said. But she didn't sound very friendly.

"Hello, Lisa," Maxine said carefully.

Maxine seemed to be waiting for a zinger. And she got one.

"I can't believe you're still in the *baby* class after all this time," said the girl named Lisa. "Babies!" She grinned nastily at Peter, Pam, and me, and walked on.

"Who does she think she is?" I said to Pam.

"I don't know," said Pam. "But she looks sort of familiar."

The second girl didn't even glance at us. She just walked right by with her nose in the air.

The first boy looked at us with an uncomfortable smile. And last came Kevin Harris. He was wearing the same nasty grin Lisa had been.

"You and your horse match, you know that, Brody?" Kevin said loudly. "You're both fat and bald!"

Okay, so I had thought the same thing. At least I had kept it to myself.

"Shut up!" Peter growled.

"Kevin, knock it off!" said an older guy. He was obviously the intermediate group's instructor. He looked tough enough to handle Kevin or anybody else.

Peter was red again.

I glanced over at Maxine. She was patting her horse as though she didn't care what Lisa had said to her. But she was chewing on her bottom lip the way I do when I'm upset.

"That girl Lisa has to be Kevin's sister, right?" I asked Peter. "She's as awful as he is."

"Yup. She was in my fourth-grade class last year. She acts like she knows everything," Peter said. He made a face. "The snobby one is her best friend, Sally Keller."

"Who's the other boy?" Pam asked.

"Don't know him," Peter said.

Diana was back with our saddles and bridles. "Has Lisa been giving you a hard time again?" she asked Maxine.

Maxine shrugged unhappily, but she didn't tattle.

Diana looked mad. "Don't pay any attention to what Lisa Harris says," Diana told the rest of us. "Lisa's just jealous because Maxine can do things in a month that took her six months to learn."

I was beginning to get the idea that maybe Maxine really was good at riding.

Diana gave each of us a saddle. We threw saddle pads on the horses' backs and started to saddle up.

Peter put a saddle pad on Hogan's back and smoothed it down.

Hogan curved his neck around. He grabbed the saddle pad between his teeth. He waved it in the air. And he threw it on the ground!

"Look at this!" Peter called.

Pam, Maxine, and I all cracked up.

"Very funny!" Peter said, disgusted. "This is a clown horse—he belongs in a circus!"

I thought Hogan looked very proud of himself.

Not Ranger. He stood like a statue until I was done.

Next, Diana handed out the bridles. "To bridle a horse, first you put the bit in its mouth," she told us. "The bit is a metal bar that helps you steer the horse. Push it gently against your horse's teeth. . . ."

"Gross—Hogan's slobbering on me," Peter grumbled.

He wiped his hand on his pants. Then I saw him dig into his pocket and slip Hogan a sour ball.

"I think he's hungry," Peter said when he saw me looking at him.

I watched Pam press the bar against Gracie's teeth. But the more she pushed, the higher Gracie raised her head. Her teeth seemed to be locked together.

"There's a trick you can use," Diana told Pam. "Maxine, would you like to show Pam when you're finished with Winnie?"

Maxine had already slipped the bit into Winnie's mouth. She had pulled the leather headpiece up over Winnie's ears. She was buckling the strap under Winnie's throat.

But I'd done all that, too, even quicker than Maxine had. I felt as though I had bridled Ranger a hundred times!

And I had seen the trick about the bit on a horse video my mother had rented for me.

"I know!" I said. "You push the bit against Gracie's teeth. Then you bend your finger—right hand—and press it against her jaw," I said to Pam.

"Good, Jessie!" Diana said. "You really have done your homework."

"Where do I push?" Pam was poking at the side of Gracie's mouth. But she wasn't pushing hard enough. She was looking anxiously at Gracie's big, yellow teeth.

"Can you tell her, Jessie?" Diana asked.

"Sure," I said. "Higher—there's an empty space between Gracie's front and back teeth."

Pam pressed her finger against Gracie's jaw again. The horse's mouth opened just enough for Pam to slide in the bit.

"It worked!" said Pam. "Thanks, Jessie."

"No problem," I said. I felt like a riding instructor!

"Now can I get on?" I asked Diana.

Diana shook her head. "Not today. Today is just to let you and your horse get to know each other. Don't forget—you'll be working as a team. Your horse has to trust you, and you have to trust him."

I groaned. I was ready to ride—I didn't care about getting to know Ranger. After all, Sasha was the horse I really needed to make friends with. Sasha and I would be winning all sorts of ribbons together soon!

"It will all happen tomorrow, Jessie," Diana said with a smile. She gave me a hug. "You're doing *great*!"

6

I was so excited about that first lesson, I practically floated through the rest of the day.

All the beginners had crafts in the Red Barn that afternoon. We started making braided riding crops. Riding crops look like little wands—you tap your horse with a crop to get his attention. But I kept messing up my braiding. All I could think about was how it would feel to ride Sasha!

Mr. Werner picked Pam and me up at four o'clock. I was so excited that I could hardly wait to get home and tell my parents all about pony camp—and about Sasha.

On the way back to Westbrook, Pam tried to tell me to take it slow. "Like your mom said, Jessie, riding isn't easy. There are lots of steps for us to learn before we can even think about hard stuff, like jumping. And Mr. Morgan said it would be at least a year before you could ride Sasha."

"But Pam, I already know so much about riding," I said. "I feel as though I've been doing it for years!"

When I got home, Mom and Dad were waiting to hear all about pony camp.

"It was . . . it was . . . *excellent*!" I said. "Diana thinks I'm doing great! I'll be jumping in no time."

I was on top of the world! Or on top of Sasha, at least in my mind. Now I knew a *real* black horse to dream about.

I did dream about him that night. Sasha and I were eventing, galloping across the countryside, jumping high fences, swimming across rivers, climbing steep hills.

Far behind us were Maxine and Winnie. And far behind them were Lisa Harris and her horse.

Pam and Peter Brody were nowhere in sight. Neither was Ranger. In my dream, it was just Sasha and me, working as a team.

But it was *Ranger* I faced at Horizon Hills the next morning. Not Sasha.

Pam, Peter, Maxine, and I stood next to our horses at one end of an outdoor riding ring.

"Everyone pay attention!" Diana said. "Jessie, I'll start with you. Let me give you a leg up."

Diana grabbed the bottom of my left leg. She gave me a boost . . . and there I was, high in the saddle, looking down at Ranger's spotted neck and shoulders!

"Now pick up the reins, Jessie," Diana said.

The reins are the leather straps that you steer a horse with. They are hooked at one end to the bit in the horse's mouth. At the other end, they are held by the rider.

"Your hands should be about four inches apart, just above Ranger's neck," Diana went on. "Don't pull the reins too tight, but they shouldn't hang loosely, either—that's right."

I had a rein in each hand. My legs were pressed against Ranger's round sides.

"Finally! I'm riding," I said. I felt like shouting it!

"Almost," said Diana. "Let's just say you're on your way."

She turned away to help Pam get settled on Gracie.

I closed my eyes for just a second. I imagined myself sailing over that stone fence in the field out front. . . .

I raised myself up in the stirrups the way riders do when they're coming to a jump. . . .

Suddenly the reins jerked forward! And so did I!

"Heeeelp!" I yelled.

I found myself halfway out of the saddle. I

had to hug Ranger's neck to keep from crashing to the ground!

"Wow!" Peter Brody said.

Now *I* thought I looked like a total dork, hanging on to Ranger's mane.

Diana grabbed me before I fell all the way off. She helped me crawl back into the saddle.

All the kids around me were nice about it. Nobody laughed.

Nobody, that is, except Kevin and Lisa Harris, who were at the other end of the outdoor ring. Some of the intermediate campers were down there doing figure eights on their horses. Kevin and Lisa were both pointing at me and cracking up.

I was ready to die of embarrassment!

"Keep your knees pressed closer to the saddle, Jessie," Diana said. In a low voice, she added, "Better keep your eyes open, too."

Then Diana went on with the lesson. "Maxine, your turn," she said.

Maxine swung onto Winnie on her own. And I had to admit, it seemed totally natural for her.

Once Peter was settled on Hogan, we were ready to walk forward.

"You should be looking straight ahead, just between your horse's ears," Diana said. "All set?"

The four of us nodded.

"Squeeze with your legs," Diana said.

I was starting to get my breath back. My head was up, my eyes straight ahead. I squeezed Ranger with my lower legs.

Ranger stepped forward. I rocked from side to side with the saddle.

"We're walking!" Peter said excitedly.

"So are we!" said Pam.

So were Ranger and I.

But I couldn't enjoy it—I was furious!

I didn't know who made me madder— Kevin and Lisa Harris, for laughing at me, or Ranger, for giving them something to laugh at! Plus, I couldn't relax. I was sure Ranger was just waiting to fake me out again. This time, I would be ready. I wouldn't fall out of the saddle again. But I was concentrating so hard that I was as stiff as a board.

"Jessie, I think you're trying too hard," Maxine said softly. "Loosen up a little. You have to be able to move with your horse."

"Yeah, sure," I snapped. Easy for her to say—she wasn't riding a horse who was out to get her!

We all walked about a third of the way across the ring.

Then Diana called from behind us, "Everybody get ready to stop. Brace yourselves and pull back evenly on the reins."

I never thought I would be glad to stop riding.

But I was glad that day. I couldn't wait to get off the horse that made me look like a beginner.

7

I didn't say anything to my parents about my accident. I acted as if I couldn't be happier about pony camp.

Every time they asked me about the camp, I'd say, "It's just great."

What else could I tell them? "I'm the biggest dork at Horizon Hills"?

Not after raving about horses for eight and a half years!

Anyway, the truth was, I blamed Ranger for my problems. I had gotten stuck with a terrible horse. Why else would he have embarrassed me like that? *I* knew all about riding from my books, so it had to be Ranger who didn't know what he was doing.

As I said to Pam the next day, "With that many horses in the barn, there has to be at least one bummer, right?"

Pam nodded.

"They wouldn't give a bummer to an intermediate or advanced rider. They would give him to a beginner who didn't know anything. And I got him."

Nothing else made sense.

"You know I'm always great at sports," I added. "Riding is a sport, and so I should be great at riding, too."

"Maybe you're expecting it to be easier than it is," Pam said. "Learning to ride is going to take some time."

"I already know how to ride, Pam," I said. "It's Ranger's fault—he messes me up."

He messed me up plenty.

At the end of the first week, Diana said we were ready for the sitting trot.

We had already learned to keep our heels

down when we rode and to keep our toes up. We had learned how to start our horses, stop them, even turn them. I *seemed* to be doing okay.

But I sure didn't *feel* right. I felt stiff and unsure of myself.

Maxine kept trying to help me. "You're doing fine, Jessie," she told me. "Just relax so that you can feel Ranger move."

"Yeah, right," I said under my breath. "Relax so he can move me right off him again."

"No, relax so you can see the signals Ranger's giving you," Maxine said.

I didn't know what she was talking about. The only signal Ranger was giving me was that he didn't like me.

On Friday morning, Diana asked Maxine, "Would you like to show us the sitting trot?"

Maxine walked Winnie out of line. Then she squeezed her legs tighter against Winnie's sides.

Winnie's head raised up higher. Her right

front leg and left back leg stepped forward at the same time—then the left front and right back leg.

Maxine swayed from side to side, and she was also rocking back and forth. She and Winnie looked as if they were joined at the saddle.

"That is so cool!" Pam said.

"It looks awfully bumpy," Peter said with a frown. "But it might be fun," he added. Peter seemed to like riding.

"Why don't you go next, Jessie?" asked Diana.

"All right," I said.

Maybe I could do it. The sitting trot would lead to the canter and then the gallop . . . and away from Ranger and on to Sasha!

First Diana hooked a long strap to Ranger's bridle.

"I'll move Ranger forward," she told me. "All you have to think about this first time is keeping your balance."

"Okay," I said.

"Shorten your reins, because Ranger's head will come up in a trot," said Diana. "Keep your back straight."

Diana jogged forward herself, tugging on Ranger. "Lean forward," she called back to me. "That will help the horse get going."

I leaned forward. I was expecting the trot to feel like a walk, only faster. But instead of just swaying from side to side, I was bouncing every which way!

So I tried to lean forward even more . . . but it was too far forward.

I was going to lose my balance! I tried to sit back in the saddle, but it was too late. Ranger suddenly stopped dead in his tracks.

"Oh, no!" I groaned just before I shot out of the saddle.

I grabbed for Ranger's neck, like the last time.

Ranger jumped sideways.

I hit the ground with a thud!

For a minute or so I just lay there, the wind knocked out of me.

I felt Ranger standing over me.

He sniffed loudly at my helmet. . . .

Then Ranger blew his nose all over my shirt!

"Gross!" Peter said in the background.

"Jessie?" Pam asked anxiously. "Are you okay?"

Pam was stuck on her horse. She wasn't very good at getting off Gracie yet.

But now Diana and Maxine were kneeling next to me.

"Do you hurt anywhere?" Diana was asking.

Maxine was trying to look at my face.

I sat up. "No, I'm not hurt," I said. I felt kind of dizzy and shaken up.

Not Ranger. Ranger was fine. He was standing off to one side. He was switching his stubby tail at flies, his eyes half-shut.

"Look at him—he's glad to be rid of me!" I said angrily. "Diana, I can't keep this up."

Diana thought I meant I wanted to stop riding.

"You've only had a few lessons. Give yourself a chance, Jessie," she said.

But I was talking about Ranger. That horse was out to get me! "I don't have a chance with this horse!" I told Diana.

"Jessie, that wasn't really Ranger's fault," Diana said. "You were leaning forward—"

"You said to lean forward," I pointed out.

"Yes, but you leaned so far forward that your seat was out of the saddle. It threw you—and Ranger—off balance," said Diana.

She helped me stand up.

Maxine brushed the dirt off my clothes.

"When Ranger felt you toppling, it scared him," Diana went on. "So he ducked away from you."

Ranger—scared? I really didn't think so. "Diana, I would like another horse," I said. I was afraid I might start crying.

"Oh, Jessie . . ." Diana looked upset, too. "I think most of the beginner horses have been given to other campers."

My lip was shaking—I couldn't stop it.

"But I'll speak to Mr. Morgan about it," Diana said quickly. "He may be able to switch someone around. It might take a while."

"I hope it won't take too long. I'm getting nowhere fast on Ranger," I said.

8

Horses grazed on a hill. Three colts were kicking up their heels in the field.

Pam, Maxine, Peter, and I were sitting at a wood table under an oak tree. It was lunchtime at Horizon Hills Farm.

All the rest of the week, Pam and I had eaten lunch together, of course. But Peter Brody had gone off by himself during lunchtime. And Maxine had disappeared somewhere, too.

But I guess they were all worried about me after my latest accident. It was nice to

69

have some friends, even if Ranger wasn't one of them.

"I can't believe it," I said to the three of them. "I've wanted to learn how to ride my whole life. I finally get my chance, and I'm sure I'll be terrific, and then Ranger throws me." I sighed. "This has never happened to me before. I'm usually great at sports."

"I'm usually awful at sports," Maxine said. "That's why I try to get out of them at school. I hate when people laugh at me."

Pam caught my eye. Pam had been right— Maxine didn't mind being sweaty or dirty. She just hated looking like a geek.

"You sure aren't awful at riding," Pam said to Maxine.

"Riding is different," said Maxine. "I think it's more like ballet than like a sport."

"Ballet?" Peter cried. "Gross!"

I didn't really get it. "How do you figure it's like ballet?" I asked Maxine.

"In baseball or basketball, I'm never sure what I should be doing next. I'm just not good at hitting a baseball or shooting a basket. But I am good at ballet, and I have good posture. So I'm also good at riding, because I'm used to holding myself the right way. I'm totally confident that I'll know what to do," Maxine said.

"Yeah—but what if your horse doesn't know what to do?" I asked. I shook my head. Normally, peanut butter and raspberry jam on six-grain bread would have cheered me up a little. But not that day at Horizon Hills. I took a bite of my sandwich, and it tasted like sawdust.

"Ranger and I aren't exactly a dream team," I went on. "More like a nightmare—or a night*horse*."

"Even old Hogan hasn't turned out to be so bad," Peter said. "Want to trade half your sandwich for half of mine?"

Peter's mom had made him a light turkey on light rye, no mayo.

"You can have the whole thing," I said. "I'm not hungry."

"Thanks!" Peter scooped up the peanut-butter-and-raspberry-jam sandwich. Before he took a bite, he said, "You have one thing to be happy about. The Harrises didn't see you hit the ground."

That morning the intermediates had been trying some jumps in the other riding ring. Kevin and Lisa hadn't been around to have a good laugh when Ranger threw me off.

"I guess I should be happy about that," I admitted. Now I knew how Maxine felt about being laughed at. Suddenly I felt bad. I was one of the people who laughed at her for being clumsy at other sports. And Maxine was being nice to me even though I was clumsy on Ranger. I would have to be nicer to Maxine, I decided. But not to Ranger.

Peter chomped down on my sandwich and chewed hungrily.

"Jessie, there's Diana!" Pam said suddenly.

"Maybe she's got some news about another horse," Maxine said.

72

When Diana walked up to us, even Peter stopped eating to listen.

"Hi, kids. Jessie, Mr. Morgan has come up with something else for you to ride," Diana said. "Want to take a look?"

"Absolutely!" I said, jumping up from the table. "What color is he? Is he tall? Is he—"

All four of us were hurrying after her toward the barn.

"No, he's not tall," Diana said. "He's part Shetland."

"Part Shetland?" I repeated. Shetlands are *tiny*.

"He belonged to Mr. Morgan's daughter Amy when she was a little girl," said Diana. "His name is Pony, and—"

"Pony? That's a dumb name," Peter said.

"Amy was only three when she named him that," Diana explained. "Pony is very quiet and—"

"Very short and very old," I interrupted. "Right?"

"Well . . ." Diana opened a stall door.

Inside was a furry white pony about half as tall as Ranger. When he saw us, he smacked his lips together.

"He's looking for a treat," Diana said.

"I've got some sour balls," said Peter, digging into his pocket.

"Oooh—he's so cute!" said Pam. "He looks like a stuffed animal."

"He's missing some teeth," Maxine said quietly.

Pony's shoulder wasn't much higher than my waist. "I can't ride him," I groaned. "My feet would drag on the ground!"

"Then you wouldn't have so far to fall!" yelled Kevin Harris. I turned to see him peering over the stable wall.

I guess Kevin had heard about my latest accident.

"BUZZ OFF, KEVIN!" Peter shouted, so loudly that all of us, including Pony, jumped.

"Yeah, Kevin! We don't need your advice," Maxine added.

"Don't you have somewhere to go?" Diana asked sharply.

"Okay, okay. I'm just trying to help," Kevin said. He strolled off, snickering.

"There are no other horses around?" I asked Diana.

"Mr. Morgan is working on it," she said. "If you don't want to try Pony, I'm afraid you'll have to deal with Ranger a while longer."

We had swimming that afternoon.

The pool at Horizon Hills is beautiful. There are big flat stones all around it, and a huge rock to dive from. From the deep end, you can see the barn and the outdoor riding rings and, way past that, Jamesport Bay.

I love to swim. An afternoon in the pool should have cheered me up. But seeing the barn in the distance reminded me of Ranger. My mood went from bad to worse.

Then Kevin Harris started giving Peter a hard time. "I'll race you, Bullethead!" he yelled. "And you can have a head start. I mean, you must have problems doing anything besides floating."

I was sitting on the edge of the pool with Pam and Maxine. We were dangling our feet in the water and talking.

"Do you hear that loudmouth?" I asked, frowning.

"Who could help it?" said Pam.

"What a bully!" said Maxine.

"You're so fat, you could *be* a float!" Kevin teased Peter.

"That does it!" I said. "I'm sick of them picking on us!"

I dove into the water. I reached Peter and Kevin in about three strokes.

"Our group against yours!" I said, getting right in Kevin's face. "A relay race."

"I bet you swim like you ride," Kevin said, cackling. "Get real."

"You're just afraid we'll win. We'll give *you* a head start!" I said.

"Racing four babies, with a head start?"

Kevin looked surprised. "What's the catch? I have to swim blindfolded and backward?"

"You're so funny, I forgot to laugh," Peter growled.

Lisa swam up to us. "You're on," she said to me. "When?"

"In ten minutes, near the diving rock," I said.

Kevin and Lisa grinned at us and swam away.

Peter grabbed my arm. He looked really worried. "Kevin is a good swimmer," he said. "And I'm not."

"You'll be fine," I promised him. "I'm fast, and so is Pam. It's going to be great to do something I'm good at again! Let's go tell Pam and Maxine."

Pam was excited, too. "We'll swim their pants off!" she said.

But Maxine wasn't so sure. "I could lose the race for us," she said. "I'm not a very good swimmer."

"You just need some confidence," I told her. "I'll help you with your swimming, and you can help me with my riding. Come on, we'll practice our strokes. And those Harrises won't know what hit them!"

9

As Pam and I helped Maxine practice her strokes, I could see Kevin, Lisa, and the other two kids in their group. They were together in a corner of the pool, planning their strategy.

"Maybe we should make a plan, too," Pam said.

We decided that Peter would swim the first two lengths of the pool.

"I want to get it over with," Peter told us.

Then Pam would swim the second lengths. Maxine would take the third.

And I would finish up.

We were ready when Kevin and Lisa swam over to us.

"You could use a few more years of practice," Kevin sneered.

"We're ready right now!" Pam replied.

"We'll give you a ten-second head start," Lisa said.

"No way will we need that," I said.

Lisa's friend Sally rolled her eyes and laughed. Lisa and Kevin laughed, too. The other boy in their group looked embarrassed by the way they were acting.

He frowned when Kevin said to us, "What do you want to bet on this race?"

"This is supposed to be fun," the boy said to Kevin.

"He is definitely cool!" Pam whispered to me.

"How about, whoever loses has to groom the other team's horses for a week?" Lisa said. "I get Maxine for my horse!" she added quickly.

I couldn't believe how awful Lisa was. I

decided Diana must be right—Lisa was jealous of Maxine.

"In your dreams!" I said to Lisa. "More like Maxine gets *you*!"

Kevin slapped his hands together. "Let's get this show on the road!" he ordered.

"Windbag!" Peter muttered.

"Kevin can't stand it when he's not the big cheese," Maxine said.

In Kevin's group the lineup would be Sally Keller, then Lisa, then the other boy, and Kevin at the end.

I would be swimming against Kevin.

When our two groups lined up at the edge of the deep end, all the other campers were watching.

"Oh, no! We have an audience," Maxine groaned. She seemed really nervous.

"Don't look at them," I told her. "And remember to breathe once in a while!"

Lisa asked the lifeguard to say "One, two, three . . . go!"

And we were off!

Peter belly-flopped when he hit the water. But he swam well. He finished only a stroke or so behind Sally Keller.

Pam more than made up for it. She has an excellent racing dive. She also has a great crawl.

Pam touched the edge of the pool a couple of yards ahead of Lisa. Then it was Maxine's turn.

Maxine's dive wasn't bad. And she stroked and kicked really hard. I was afraid she would wear herself out before she could finish.

But Maxine held her own against the boy for a length and a half of the pool.

Then he pulled ahead of her.

So Kevin Harris hit the water before I did.

His arms were churning the water like a motor.

I didn't let it get me frazzled, though. I worked on keeping up an even stroke and even breathing. I paced myself.

I knew I was a stronger swimmer than

Kevin. The gap between us was closing.

Because Kevin is such a loudmouth, he's not popular. I could hear a lot of kids cheering for me even though they didn't know my name yet.

"Faster, you can beat him!"

"He's getting tired."

"You've got him now!"

About halfway through the second length of the pool, Kevin began to slow down. He had burned himself out.

That's when I gave it everything I had!

I shot through the water ahead of Kevin. My hand slapped the edge of the pool two seconds before Kevin's did!

When I climbed out of the water, all the kids cheered for me. Peter was doing a victory dance on the edge of the pool. "We won!" he yelled happily.

"I think that's the first time I've ever won anything. In sports, I mean," Maxine said.

"Way to go!" Pam said to me.

We gave each other high fives. Then we

gave Maxine and Peter high fives. "Dream Team!" we yelled.

The boy from Kevin's group swam over to us. "Hi, I'm Bill Frano," he said. "Great race."

Kevin, Lisa, and Sally were standing near the diving rock, looking bummed out.

"Hey, Kevin," Peter called over to them. "On Monday you can groom Hogan."

"And Lisa can groom Winnie!" Maxine said quietly.

"See? All you needed was some confidence," I said to Maxine.

"You were right," Maxine said. "And that's all you need for your riding, too."

"And a horse that isn't a dud," Peter added.

That made me think of Ranger again. But even though Ranger was still a dud, I felt better now. Pam, Peter, and even Maxine were on my side—after the swimming race, we were really a team! Maybe Maxine could even help me with Ranger. . . .

"Time to change out of your bathing suits," the lifeguard called.

So we headed for the dressing rooms.

Peter was waiting for us after we had changed.

"I have to show you something," he said. He sounded really excited.

"My mom is going to be here any second," I told him.

"Can't it wait?" Pam asked.

Peter shook his head. "No! It's important for Jessie."

"For me?" I said. What could it be?

"Come *on*," said Peter.

There was another riding ring behind the barn. A line of wood jumps was set up in it—high jumps, wide jumps, and all sorts of combinations.

"Look! That's a jump just like the one at the horse show on TV," Pam pointed out. "It even has the same row of flowers on the bottom."

Peter sighed loudly. "Don't look at the

jump!" he said. "Look at the horse!"

At the far end of the ring stood a horse and rider. The horse was black—in spots. He was also white—in spots.

"Ranger!" I exclaimed.

"Watch!" said Peter.

As we watched, the rider cantered Ranger around the ring.

"Jessie, it's Sara, the dressage girl!" Pam said as they passed us.

"Sssh," said Peter.

Sara straightened Ranger out.

She aimed him at the first jump.

Ranger gathered himself. . . .

Sara leaned closer to his neck. . . .

Ranger took off. He sailed over the jump as though he had wings!

He cantered to the next jump, the one with flowers. He cleared it with a yard to spare!

Ranger took all the jumps in stride, without a slip.

Sara cantered him around the ring once more. Then she slowed him to a walk. She patted Ranger's neck and spoke quietly to him.

Diana walked up behind us.

"What did you think of that?" Diana asked me.

"I can't believe it! Ranger is fantastic!" I said.

"I know he is," Diana said with a smile. "Sara has won a lot of ribbons with Ranger. Do you still want to trade him in for another horse?"

I shook my head. "No way—Ranger is sure good enough for me! And I hope I can be good enough for him!"

"That's the spirit!" said Diana. "Now I have something else to show all of you. Jane the cat just had three kittens in Gracie's stall!"

The next week, Kevin, Lisa, and Sally groomed our horses every morning. Pam didn't think it was fair to make Bill Frano groom hers, because he was so nice. So Pam and Bill groomed Gracie together.

Otherwise, things at Horizon Hills seemed

the same. But they were totally different—for me, anyway.

Sure, Pam was riding Gracie, Peter was riding Hogan, and Maxine was riding Winnie. And I was riding Ranger.

But now, instead of thinking about how much *I* knew, I was thinking about how much *Ranger* knew. I mean, he had been doing this stuff for years. I had only been doing it for five days! And now that I knew how terrific Ranger was, I wanted to work hard to be a good enough rider for him. After all, a great horse deserves a great rider!

And I had already learned two things at pony camp. Number one, that I had tons more to learn about riding. And number two, that everything is easier when you're part of a team. I had Pam, Peter, and Maxine on my team. Pam kept me from getting too far ahead of myself. Peter showed me that anyone can improve if you try hard enough. And Maxine gave me plenty of tips about horses.

Diana was still saying things like, "We're

going to turn right. Look to the right. Move your right leg forward a bit, move your left leg back. . . ."

But I had changed. Now I was part of another team, too.

That team was me and Ranger.

I was learning how to understand his signals—like one spotted ear pointed forward and the other pointed back at me. In horse talk, that meant, "What's going on? How are you doing up there?"

When Diana asked me to demonstrate my sitting trot, I squeezed my legs against Ranger's sides and leaned forward a little. That told Ranger I wanted him to go faster.

When he started to trot, I kept my legs close to the saddle. I stayed centered.

I didn't lean too much. I didn't bounce all over the place. And I didn't fall off!

"It's working!" I yelled to Diana.

And I was happy to be able to tell Ranger, "So far, we're doing just fine!"